W9-AYI-145

Dear Parent:
Your child's love of reading starts here!

Every child learns to read in a different way and at his or her own speed. Some go back and forth between reading levels and read favorite books again and again. Others read through each level in order. You can help your young reader improve and become more confident by encouraging his or her own interests and abilities. From books your child reads with you to the first books he or she reads alone, there are I Can Read Books for every stage of reading:

SHARED READING
Basic language, word repetition, and whimsical illustrations, ideal for sharing with your emergent reader

BEGINNING READING
Short sentences, familiar words, and simple concepts for children eager to read on their own

READING WITH HELP
Engaging stories, longer sentences, and language play for developing readers

READING ALONE
Complex plots, challenging vocabulary, and high-interest topics for the independent reader

ADVANCED READING
Short paragraphs, chapters, and exciting themes for the perfect bridge to chapter books

I Can Read Books have introduced children to the joy of reading since 1957. Featuring award-winning authors and illustrators and a fabulous cast of beloved characters, I Can Read Books set the standard for beginning readers.

A lifetime of discovery begins with the magical words "I Can Read!"

Visit www.icanread.com for information
on enriching your child's reading experience.

ADVENTURES OF
ICE AGE™

An Imprint of Sterling Publishing
387 Park Avenue South
New York, NY 10016

ADVENTURES OF ICE AGE

This 2013 edition published by Sandy Creek by
arrangement with HarperCollins Publishers.

ISBN 978-1-4351-5060-7

Manufactured in Dong Guan City, China
Lot #:
13 14 15 16 17 SCP 5 4 3 2 1
08/13

An I Can Read Book™

ADVENTURES OF
ICE AGE™

Sandy Creek
NEW YORK

Table of Contents

ICE AGE 2™
THE MELTDOWN

GEYSER BLAST!

Adapted by Ellie O'Ryan
Illustrated by Artful Doodlers, UK

Welcome to the Ice Age—
a time when the world was frozen.
Many animals lived on the ice,
like Manny and his friends
Sid and Diego.

One day, Manny saw something strange.

The ice was melting.

"It is going to flood!" he yelled.

Soon their home would be covered

with water.

Sid suggested becoming water creatures.

"Genius," Diego said, rolling his eyes.

But Sid had a point—land animals

cannot live in an underwater world.

It was time to find a new home—fast.

The friends heard about a giant boat.

It was really far away, but it would

take them to dry land.

Manny, Sid, and Diego decided

to travel in search of the boat.

Along the way, they met Ellie
and her brothers, Crash and Eddie.
The group did not all get along at first.
But they soon realized that it would
take teamwork to get where they all
were going.

Look! Diego saw the boat.

Everyone cheered.

The gang would be saved, and

they had gotten there together.

As the group celebrated their journey, a geyser exploded nearby. Sid was not worried, though. "It is just a little water and steam. How bad could it be?" Sid asked.

Just then a dodo bird sat near Sid.

Whoosh—a geyser blew under the bird!

Boiling water and steam shot
into the sky.

Feathers flew everywhere.

Good-bye, dodo!

Now Sid was worried.

The pressure was too much for Eddie.

"I am too young to die!" he screamed.

"Actually, possums do not
live very long," Crash replied.
"So you're kind of due."
"Ahhhhhh!" wailed Eddie.

Finally, Ellie stepped in to

calm her brothers down.

"Nobody is going to die!" Ellie said.

Manny looked around.

He did not see Ellie anywhere.

Then he looked up.

Ellie was sitting in a tree!

From up there, she saw that the geysers
were spouting in a pattern.

She had an idea.

"I can tell you which way to go!"
she said.

"No way," Manny replied.

He did not want to leave Ellie behind.

There must be another way, he thought.

But there was no other way.

"Mammoths are brave," Ellie said.

"Are you brave enough to trust me?"

"Yes," Manny replied.

He picked up Crash, Eddie, and Sid,

and put them on his back.

Then they made a run for it!

Ellie told her friends where to go.
"Left! Left! Straight!
Right! Straight! Right!
STOP!"

They made it!

"You are home free!" yelled Ellie.

But then a new problem showed itself.

One by one, more geysers erupted.

They were heading straight for

Ellie's tree!

Wham!

A geyser blew up the tree Ellie was perched in.

Where did she go?

The friends thought the worst.

Then they saw a wonderful sight—

Ellie running for safety.

Crash and Eddie ran to meet her.

Oh, no!

More geysers blew.

The ground split in two!

Manny tried to run to Ellie.

But there was too much steam

and smoke.

Manny could barely see anything.

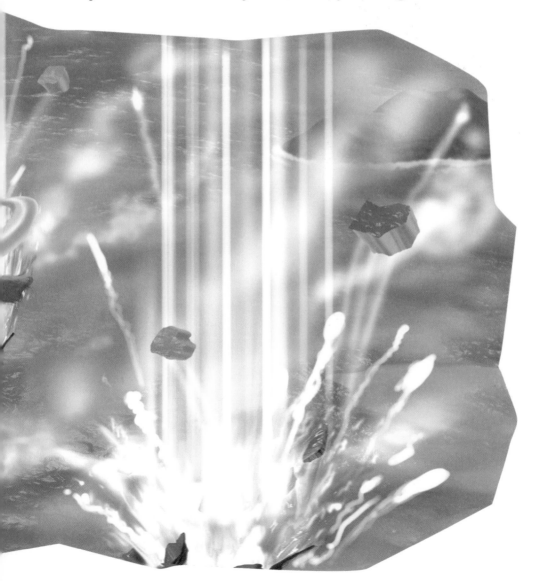

The split in the ground grew bigger.

Manny tried to jump over it—

but Diego stopped him just in time!

Finally, the geysers stopped blowing,

the crack stopped growing,

and the steam started to fade.

Sid opened his eyes.

"Are we dead?" he asked.

No—they were fine!

Where are Ellie, Crash, and Eddie?

Manny wondered.

"ELLIE!" he yelled.

Everyone waited for her to yell back.

36

"We are okay, too!" Ellie called.

She was on the other side of the crack.

Everyone cheered!

"We will meet you at the boat!"

Manny yelled.

Manny, Sid, and Diego went one way.
Ellie, Crash, and Eddie went
the other way.
"The worst is behind us,"
Manny declared.
On to the giant boat!

JOIN THE PACK!

Adapted by Ellie O'Ryan
Illustrations by Artful Doodlers, UK

Meet Manny.

He is a mammoth.

He lives on an icy glacier with his pals,
Sid the sloth and Diego the
saber-toothed tiger.

Sid runs a camp at the water park—
Campo del Sid.

That means *Camp of Sid*.

"Congratulations, now you are an idiot
in two languages!" Diego tells him.

Sid wants his friends to respect him.

So he decides to jump off the biggest

waterslide in the park!

Diego cannot believe Sid is that dumb.

Manny grabs Sid just before he jumps.

Then Manny notices something.

The glaciers are melting!

And that can mean only one thing. . . .

A flood is coming!

Sid wants to become a water creature.

"Call me Squid," he says.

When the flood comes,
everything will be under water.
The animals must leave the
glacier—fast.
It is not safe to stay where they are.

Far away, there is a giant boat.
It will take the animals to a place
where the flood will not affect them.
All the animals pack up and leave.
Manny, Sid, and Diego leave, too.

On the trip, Manny hears bad news.

Some animals tell him that mammoths
are extinct.

Manny might be the last mammoth
in the whole world.

He sees his reflection in the icicles and
wonders if it is true.
This makes Manny feel very lonely.

Manny goes for a walk to
think things over.
Suddenly, a big tree in front of him
wobbles and shakes.
There is a mammoth hanging from it!

Manny is so glad to meet a mammoth.

Her name is Ellie.

There is just one problem.

Ellie thinks she is a possum!

These are Ellie's brothers,

Crash and Eddie.

They are possums.

Manny wonders if Ellie is a little crazy.

Manny and Ellie are the same size.

They have the same footprints.

They have the same shadows.

But Ellie still does not believe

that she is a mammoth!

Manny and his pals decide to travel
with Ellie, Crash, and Eddie.
Sid thinks Manny and Ellie are
a good pair—Ellie is lots of fun
and Manny is no fun at all!

Along the way, Manny tries to show
Ellie how to use her trunk to lift things.
Ellie does not think her trunk
works that way.
She is driving Manny nuts!

Manny and Ellie find a meadow.

Ellie remembers a time long ago.

She was alone and scared

in a meadow like this one.

A family of possums found her.

They took care of her.

Suddenly, Ellie understands—
she *is* a mammoth, after all!
"A mammoth never forgets,"
Manny says.

Ellie always knew she was different.
Now everything makes sense.
She was always bigger and stronger
than her possum friends and relatives.

Mammoths are powerful.

But they are gentle, too.

Ellie woke up thinking she was a possum.

Now she knows she is a mammoth.

The friends are almost at the boat. First, they must cross a geyser field that shoots boiling water and steam. Manny and Ellie have different ideas on how to get across.

Who will the pack follow?

Time is running out—they must choose.

"We should separate," Ellie says.

They do, and make it across safely.

But Ellie, Crash, and Eddie end up

far away from the others.

"See you at the boat!" Manny yells.

On the way to the boat,

Ellie gets trapped in a cave.

Suddenly, the big flood comes!

What will happen to Ellie?

Manny will not let Ellie down.

He has a plan to save her.

Will it work?

Manny uses the power of the water
to free Ellie.

Ellie is safe!

The mammoths swirl around
in the whirlpool.
Then the water drains out.
The big flood is over.
Manny and Ellie are safe!

Manny hears something.

It is a whole herd of mammoths!

Ellie and Manny are *not* the only

ones left.

Ellie wants to go with the mammoths.

Manny wants to stay with his pals.

But he does not want Ellie to go.

He hangs from a tree like a possum.

"Ellie, wait!" he yells.

"I want to be with you!"

Manny and Ellie do not need
to join the herd.
They can make their own herd—
with Sid, Diego, Crash, and Eddie!

ICE AGE™
DAWN OF THE DINOSAURS
ALL IN THE FAMILY

Adapted by Sierra Harimann

Manny was excited.

He was going to be a dad.

Ellie was Manny's wife.

She was going to have a baby.

Their family of mammoths

was about to grow.

Ellie and Manny lived
during the Ice Age
with all of their friends.
Their friends were family, too.
Crash and Eddie the possums
were excited about the baby.

So was Sid the sloth.

But Diego the saber-toothed tiger

wasn't sure how he felt.

One day,

Manny wanted to surprise Ellie

with a gift.

He invited everyone to see it.

"Can I look now?" asked Ellie.

"Now!" said Manny.

Manny had made a pretty mobile
from the ice crystal.
Manny, Ellie, and the baby
were on the mobile.
"It's our family," said Manny.
"It's amazing," said Ellie.

Just then, Ellie felt the baby move.

"What's happening?" said Manny.

"Are you having the baby?

Take a deep breath.

Nobody else breathe!"

"It was just a kick," said Ellie.

"Manny, you've got to relax,"
said Ellie.

"The best way to protect our baby
is to have our friends around us."
Then Ellie realized something.
Where was Diego?

Diego was far away,
chasing a gazelle.

Diego was not thinking about babies.

He did not care about mobiles.

Diego wanted a life of adventure.

When Diego finally showed up,
he told Manny how he felt.
"I'm happy for you," he said,
"but having a family is
your adventure, not mine."

"It might be time for me
to head out on my own," said Diego.
Manny was hurt.
He thought Diego didn't want to be
part of the family anymore.

"Well, go find some adventure,
Mr. Adventure Guy," said Manny.
"Don't let my boring life
hit you on the way out."

Sid tried to stop Diego from going.

"We're a herd. A family!" he said.

"Things have changed," said Diego.

Diego didn't think anything
could make him stick around.
But when he heard
that the baby was on its way,
something inside him changed.

Diego wanted to be there for Ellie.
He wanted to celebrate with Sid,
Manny, and all of his friends.
Maybe having a baby in the family
would be its own great adventure.

Soon, the baby was born.

It was a girl!

"Welcome to the Ice Age, sweetie,"

said Ellie.

"She's beautiful," Sid said.
"I'm glad she looks like Ellie.
No offense, Manny."

"Thanks for coming back,"
Manny told Diego.
"I know this baby stuff
isn't for you."

Diego smiled.

He had made an important decision.

"I'm not leaving, buddy,"

Diego said to Manny.

"All the adventure I want

is right here," said Diego.

"I couldn't leave my family."

Manny was glad

to have his friend back.

Everyone cheered with joy.

They were a family again!

The baby settled down for a nap.

She had two loving parents

and a big family of friends.

What more could a mammoth want?

MANNY'S BIG ADVENTURE

Written by J. E. Bright

A loud rumble woke Manny the mammoth.

He checked on his wife, Ellie,

and his teenage daughter, Peaches.

Ellie was fine.

Peaches was missing!

Peaches had gone to the Falls, a teen hangout.

Manny was furious.

"You're overreacting," said Ellie.

"She won't be your little girl forever."

Manny said, "That's what worries me."

Her mother, Ellie,

was raised by possums.

She could hang from tree branches

by her tail.

Peaches also slept hanging upside down.

That's how her friend Louis,

a molehog, found her before

they went to the Falls.

"We shouldn't risk death," said Louis,

"so you can meet a cute mammoth."

Peaches said, "You can't live life

by playing it safe."

Manny snuck up behind Peaches.

"I know I would," he said.

"Dad," said Peaches, "don't be mad."

Manny grunted.

"You know how I feel
about you going to the Falls alone."

"She's not alone, sir," said Louis.

"You don't count," replied Manny.

Manny led Peaches away.

"We're going home," he said,

"where I can keep an eye on you."

Another rumble shook the ground,

scaring Louis back to his hole.

Despite her father's warnings,

Peaches and Louis snuck to the Falls.

They found a teen party!

"Look!" Peaches said to Louis.

"There's Ethan!"

Peaches tripped, sliding down the ice!

She plummeted into the valley

and slammed into Ethan.

Their tusks tangled together.

At that moment, Manny appeared again.

"Am I interrupting something?"

he said angrily.

Peaches and Ethan tried

to untangle their tusks.

Manny yanked them apart.

"Keep away from my daughter!"

he said, growling at Ethan.

Then he told Peaches, "You're grounded!"

Embarrassed, Peaches stormed away.

Manny hurried after Peaches.

"Let's talk about this!" he said.

Peaches yelled, "I'm not a kid!

You can't control my life!"

That hurt Manny's feelings.

Peaches hurried away past Ellie.

"She doesn't mean it, honey,"

Ellie told Manny soothingly.

A huge rumble shook the earth.

Sid the sloth held his stomach.

"Whoa," he said. "Excuse me."

"I don't think that was you," said Diego
the saber-toothed tiger.

A crack split the icy ground

between Manny and his wife and daughter.

"Manny!" Ellie screamed. "No!"

"Peaches!" yelled Manny. "Get back!"

Sid and Diego grabbed onto Manny.

The ice shelf they stood on

slid into the water of the bay!

Manny ran along the edge of the ice,

looking for a place to jump.

"Hurry, Dad!" Peaches shouted.

Manny crouched to leap

across the icy water.

Diego stopped Manny from jumping.

"You won't make it!" said Diego.

The continent was crumbling!

"Go to the land bridge!" yelled Manny.

"You'll be safe on the other side!"

The broken ice shelf carried

Manny, Diego, and Sid out to sea.

"Daddy!" Peaches screamed.

Manny shouted, "I will find you!

No matter how long it takes."

"It's all my fault," wailed Peaches.

"If I had listened to him—"

Ellie said, "It's not your fault."

"But the last thing we did

was fight." Peaches sobbed.

"Your father is the toughest, most stubborn mammoth I know," said Ellie. "He'll come back for us. That's a promise."

Manny, Sid, and Diego floated

out onto the ocean.

They barely survived a wild storm.

"We have each other," said Sid.

"Things could be worse, right?"

Then they discovered a stowaway.

It was Sid's granny!

"Have you seen Precious?" asked Granny.

"You mean your imaginary pet?"
replied Diego. "No, I haven't."

Then Manny, Sid, and Diego

got into a sea battle with pirates.

They escaped on their melting iceberg.

"We'll never get home

on this thing," said Diego.

"Land!" cried Manny.

They had found an island . . .

but it was the pirate hideout!

They had to stop there—

the iceberg wouldn't last any longer.

On the pirate's island,
they discovered a fast current
called Switchback Cove.
"That's the way home!" said Manny.
Sid said, "But we need a ship."

Manny pointed at the pirates' ice ship.

Although the pirates swore revenge,

Manny, Diego, and Sid stole the ship!

The strong current carried them

back toward Manny's family.

After sailing a long time,

Manny spotted land again.

"We're almost home!" He cheered.

"I never doubted you," said Diego.

"Me either," said Sid.

But the pirates got there first!

They grabbed Ellie and Peaches.

Manny thought all was lost.

Then Precious, Granny's real pet whale,

showed up to help save everybody!

Manny and his friends and family

sailed to a beautiful new land.

Manny, Ellie, and Peaches hugged.

"I love you, Dad," said Peaches.